MARK ™

THE MOUNTAIN GUIDE

AND THE COMPASS ADVENTURE

S0-ABB-296

BOXER BOOKS

WRITTEN BY
MARK SEATON

ILLUSTRATED BY
GRAHAM PHILPOT

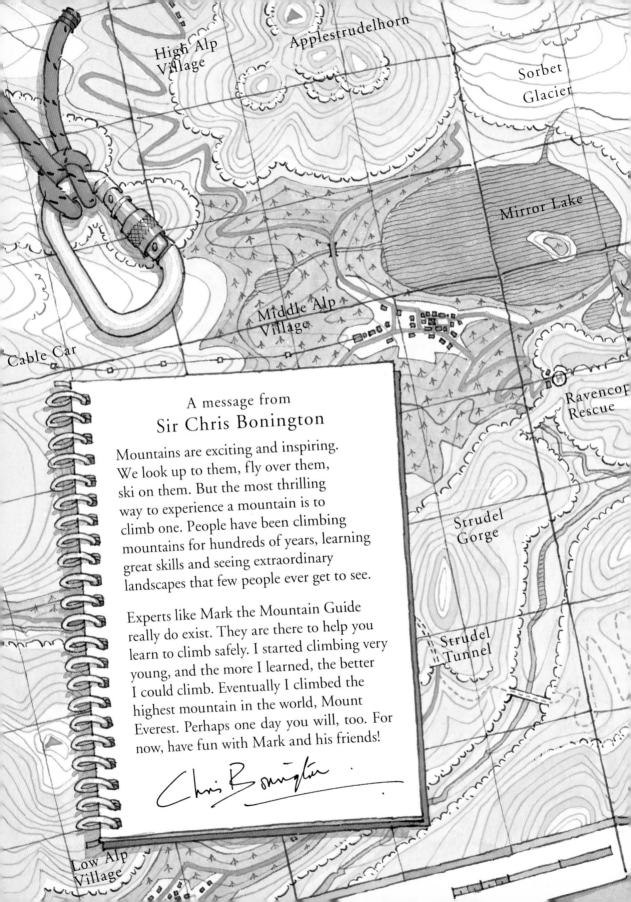

High Alp
Village

Applestrudelhorn

Sorbet
Glacier

Mirror Lake

Cable Car

Middle Alp
Village

Ravencop
Rescue

A message from
Sir Chris Bonington

Mountains are exciting and inspiring.
We look up to them, fly over them,
ski on them. But the most thrilling
way to experience a mountain is to
climb one. People have been climbing
mountains for hundreds of years, learning
great skills and seeing extraordinary
landscapes that few people ever get to see.

Experts like Mark the Mountain Guide
really do exist. They are there to help you
learn to climb safely. I started climbing very
young, and the more I learned, the better
I could climb. Eventually I climbed the
highest mountain in the world, Mount
Everest. Perhaps one day you will, too. For
now, have fun with Mark and his friends!

Chris Bonington

Strudel
Gorge

Strudel
Tunnel

Low Alp
Village

Mark the Mountain Guide had been sawing, banging and painting in his workshop for days. Mary Marmot and the three little marmot mountaineers stood outside with Epic Eddy and Leo the Mountain Dog, waiting impatiently. "What can he be doing?" asked Mary.

"Phew, finished at last!" said Mark as he dragged a huge,
strange-looking box out of his workshop.

"What is it?" asked Leo the Mountain Dog.

But before Mark could answer . . .

BANG! Two doors burst open and a giant bird came flying out of the box on the end of a long spring.

Cuckoo!

"I'm Cuckoo," announced the funny-looking bird, "and THIS is a Cuckoo Clock!"

Cuckoo! Cuckoo!

Then he shot back inside the box, and the doors slammed shut.

"EPIC!" said Eddy, shaking his head in disbelief.

"Does he have a volume button?" asked Leo the Mountain Dog.

"He's only supposed to say 'cuckoo' once every hour," said Mary.

"He's not supposed to talk!"

"Listen, Mountaineers," Mark continued. "Our job is to get this cuckoo clock to Middle Alp Village—today!"

Suddenly the doors shot open
again and Cuckoo shouted,
"Because I have a very
important job to do. I'm the new
Middle Alp Village town clock.
So hurry up and get me there!"

"How rude!" said Mary Marmot.
"He'll calm down once we get him to the clock tower in Middle Alp
Village," said Mark. "Now let's get going. We don't want to be late."

Together they loaded the cuckoo clock into the back of Mark's truck.
"Now drive slowly, Eddy," Mark instructed. "The road is twisty, and
there will be slippery ice and snow along the way."

Eddy started off on the steep winding road toward the pass. But as they rounded a bend, the road was blocked by a huge snowdrift. Eddy slammed on the brakes, but he couldn't stop the truck.

They slid into the giant mound of soft snow—and stuck there!

Mark surveyed the situation. "We'll never get the truck out today, so we'll have to find another way to Middle Alp Village," he said. "And we'll have to carry the cuckoo clock."

"Epic," said Eddy. "I can do that!"

Cuckoo! The doors flew open and Cuckoo cried out: "Oh, no! He's not carrying me! He'll drop me! I'm fragile, you know!"

"Calm down, Cuckoo," said Mary Marmot, handing
Mark the compass as he opened up his map.
"One!

    Two!

        Three!

Yippee! Are we lost?" added the little marmots together.

Mark showed the little marmot mountaineers his map and
compass. "We go northwest for one mile. Then we'll be at the
pass. After that, it's downhill all the way to Middle Alp Village."
"Right," said Mary, pointing northwest.
Leo led the way.

When they reached the pass, Mark said, "Let's stop to rest here.
We can have something to eat and drink."
"Epic, I'm famished!" said Eddy, swinging the clock off his back.
"Look out!" Mark warned. "The cuckoo clock is going to slide!"
Too late! Eddy had set the clock down on a slippery spot, and
it started sliding down the mountain like a toboggan.

Everyone rushed after the clock, but Mark managed
to grab it. Then he grabbed Mary's hand;
Mary grabbed Leo; Leo grabbed Eddy;
and Eddy grabbed the little marmots!

Whoosh! They hurtled down the snow-covered mountainside!
"EPIC!" shouted Eddy. "We'll be in Middle Alp Village in no time!"

"I don't think so," Mary said, peering at the compass.
"We're going north, not northwest!"
"And there's a steep cliff at the bottom of this slope!"
shouted Mark.

The cuckoo clock, with all its passengers, shot off the cliff
and they were suddenly flying through the air.
"One! Two! Three! Whee!" said the marmots.

For the second time that day, they landed in a huge snowdrift.

The doors on the clock creaked open and Cuckoo wobbled out.

"I told you he would drop me," he moaned.

"Calm down, Cuckoo," Mary soothed him. "You're fine."

Now Mark studied his map and compass.

"We're at the bottom of Deep Gorge," said Mark.

"The only way out is to climb up the cliff. So let's get going!"

Mark went up first, tying a rope around the
clock. Eddy went up behind him, the clock on
his back. Leo pushed from below. Finally, after
a lot of huffing and puffing, they all climbed
out of the gorge.

"Well done, everyone!" said Mark. "That was a good team effort."
In the distance the mountaineers could just see the village of Middle Alp.

The clock was balanced in the snow when Mary shouted,
"It's twelve o'clock! Someone stop the cuckoo!"
But she was too late . . .
Cuckoo! Cuckoo! Cuckoo-oo-oo!
Cuckoo toppled over, and the clock went
crashing down yet another slope!

The mountaineers just gaped as the cuckoo clock landed
in the river at the bottom of another deep, dark gorge.
Instantly, Mark the Mountain Guide took charge.

"Come on team! We're going to rappel down the cliff and rescue that clock," he said. He quickly organized the ropes and the mountaineers followed him over the cliff—
just in time for everyone to jump aboard!
"Wowee!" shouted the three little marmots.

"I feel sick," spluttered Cuckoo,

Cuckoo-hic! Cuckoo-hic!

"White-water rafting!" shouted Eddy. "Epic!"

The little marmots were not so sure.

"Uh-oh," said Leo, "What's that rumbling sound?"

"Hold on tight!" cried Mark.

"It's going to get a little choppy," said Mary.

"Is that a waterfall ahead?" asked Eddy excitedly.

Eddy was right. The cuckoo clock, with everyone sitting on top of it, plunged headlong over a gigantic waterfall . . .

. . . then splashed into a foaming pool at the bottom.
"Whoopee!" shouted three excited little marmots.

As Mark's mountaineers clung to the sides of the cuckoo clock,
Mark unfolded his rather wet map.

Mary Marmot peered at Mark's compass and tried to get her bearings.

"Aha! This river runs west," she cried.

"It will take us to Mirror Lake!" said Mark. "We're nearly there."

Cuckoo emerged from the side of the clock spluttering.

Just then, they heard a
helicopter overhead.
"That's my pal, Ralph Ravencopter!
He can help us," said Cuckoo.

Mark pulled his walkie-talkie out of his backpack.
"Ralph! Ralph Ravencopter! Mark the Mountain
Guide here. Do you read me? Over."
"Mark! Mark! Ralph Ravencopter here! I read you,
loud and clear. What's up down there? Over."

"What's up is we're down here! Over," said Mark.

"I'm coming straight down. Over and out," Ralph Ravencopter replied.

While Mark stayed behind to secure the cuckoo clock with ropes,

Ralph Ravencopter airlifted Mark's team to safety.

In Middle Alp Village, a large crowd
had begun to gather.
"Can you help us get Cuckoo over to
the Middle Alp Village Clock Tower?"
asked Mark. "We're running a little late."

Ralph Ravencopter went into a steep dive, swooped down,
and lowered a rope. Mark secured the rope around the clock.
Then, very slowly and expertly, Ralph flew the cuckoo clock,
with Mark on board, to the top of the tower.

At last Mark the Mountain Guide installed the clock in its proper place. Far below in the town square a loud cheer went up from the crowd. Then there was silence. At exactly one o'clock the doors flew open and Cuckoo burst out:

Cuckoo!

Then he shot back inside and the doors slammed shut. There was more cheering from the crowd, and lots of clapping. Then Cuckoo shot out again, Mark whispered, "Oh, no!" But to his relief, Cuckoo just took a bow and popped back inside without saying another word.

"Three cheers for Mark the Mountain Guide and his mountaineers!" cried a voice in the crowd.

Mark's mountaineers waved their thanks to Ralph Ravencopter.

"EPIC adventure!" said Eddy with a big smile as the team

said good-bye to Middle Alp Village.

"What was it?" asked Mark.

"It was EPIC!" they all said together,

and laughed out loud.

CUCKOO

Why put a cuckoo in a clock?

The cuckoo clock was first described about 370 years ago in Germany. We do not know why someone decided to use the call of the cuckoo bird in a clock. Maybe because it is a simple sound that can be made mechanically. Maybe the inventor just liked the sound.

Cuckoo!

The sound is made by two tiny pipes that have bellows attached. When the clock strikes the hour, the clock mechanism inside squeezes the bellows, which puff out air into one pipe, then the other, making the cuckoo sound.

The Black Forest in Germany has been famous for making cuckoo clocks for more than 250 years. They come in all sorts of designs, but the best known is the Hunter's clock. It is shaped like a house and is often decorated with carved oak leaves, guns, deer, rabbits, or game birds.

What is a compass?

A compass is a tool that tells you which direction you are going. Have a look at your compass. If you walk around with it, you will see the needle swing around as you change direction. When you stand still, the needle will settle into one position. The red end of the needle is pointing north.

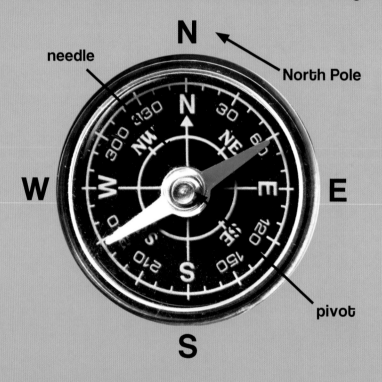

Why does the needle point north?

The needle in your compass is a magnet. Magnets are attracted to other magnetic materials and try to stick to them.

The Earth is magnetic. Think of it as having a giant magnet inside. Your compass needle swings towards the North Pole because it wants to stick to it. Because of this fact you can use your compass to help you find your way when using a map.

Earth's North Pole and South Pole are not the true magnetic poles. The magnetic poles are a little bit to the side of where we place the poles on our maps.

Compass history

The Chinese people were using magnets hundreds of years ago. They used a magnetic needle floating in a dish of water. By the 14th century the dry compass, which is the type we use today, had been invented. Legend tells that magnetism was discovered by a Greek shepherd named Magnes when he noticed that his iron-tipped crook picked up pieces of black rock called magnetite.

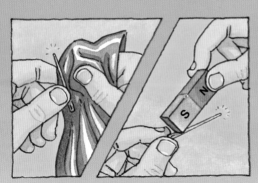 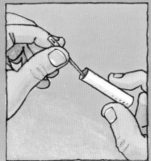 

Make your own compass!

Ask a grown-up to help you magnetize a sewing needle, but be careful not to prick your fingers! Rub the needle with silk or, if you have a magnet, stroke the south end along the pointy end of the needle a few times. Then put the needle into a short piece of cut-off drinking straw and float it in a cup of water. If you have magnetized the needle enough, the pointed end will swing around toward the north.

Make sure you have a compass with you whenever you go hiking, and make sure you know how to use it!

MAPS

What is a map?

A map is a flat diagram of a section of the Earth showing roads and rivers and other features. Do you know how to use a map? Maps have a lot of information that will help you find your way.

Contour lines tell you the height of the land. The closer together the lines are, the steeper the slope of the land.

Arrow or Compass Rose gives direction, always pointing north.

Key describes the symbols on the map, and the types of roads and highways.

Symbols tell you interesting things to explore, such as lookout points, camping grounds, picnic areas, or museums.

Scale
tells you how to measure distance on the map. Here, 1 mile on Earth is represented by 1 inch on the map.

R

S

N

T

U

Road

Track

Water

Forest

Ridge

Rest Area

Information

Rescue Point

Parking

Mark the Mountain Guide was able to keep his team on the right path to Middle Alp Village by using his compass and his map!

HOW TO RAPPEL

Rappelling—also known as abseiling—is a way of getting down a cliff or mountainside on a fixed rope. A mountain guide from the Alps invented the method over 100 years ago. Mark carried climbing rope in his backpack to secure at the top of the cliff. The climbers slide down the rope using a device called a descender. This device clips to the climber's harness and allows them to control their descent down the cliff.

A helmet and boots protect climbers from scrapes against the rock face. Rescue workers sometimes have to rappel down cliffs to reach people who are stuck.

RIVER RAFTING

Also called white-water rafting, rafting on a fast-flowing river can be great fun! You whiz down the river in an inflatable raft, getting very wet! Rafting experts who lead tour groups will make sure you have the correct gear, such as a helmet and a life jacket, in case you fall out! Tour leaders also teach groups how to paddle the raft together and guide them through the rapids, which can be dangerous. (Mark's team wasn't wearing the right gear, but they didn't know they would be rafting down a river on a cuckoo clock!)

There are many places in the world where you can go white-water rafting. From Scotland to Africa, North America to Australia, all you need is a fast-flowing river. Epic Eddy is thinking about trying it again! White-water rafting is fun, but you should only try it if you are with an experienced guide

MOUNTAIN RESCUE

Who are they?

Walking and climbing in the mountains can be risky, even if you are as experienced as Mark the Mountain Guide. The weather can change suddenly in the mountains, or you could trip and hurt yourself or get lost. Mountain rescue teams go out in all kinds of weather to save people who are in trouble. Very highly trained, the teams are often not paid, but work as volunteers!

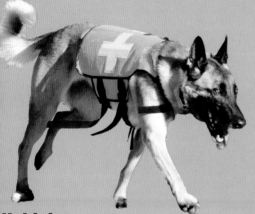

Rescue dogs

Dogs are the best at sniffing out lost people because they have such a good sense of smell. They are trained to bark for their handler when they find the lost person and lead their handler to the person who needs to be rescued.

Vehicles

Mountain rescue teams use tough 4x4 vehicles that can drive over rough ground. They carry medical equipment and stretchers to help injured people and carry them back to safety. If someone is stuck on a cliff or in the water, like Mark and his team, a helicopter can hover above them and lower a rope and harness to pull people to safety.

Mark the Mountain Guide says: Make sure you really are in trouble before you call the rescue service!

MOUNTAIN FEATURES

The mountains where Mark lives are all shapes and sizes. Some have pointy tops. Others have sharp ridges on one side with gaps. There are waterfalls, wide valleys, and rock piles. Where did all these different shapes and features come from? Long ago, during the last ice age, the area where Mark lives became covered with lakes of ice called glaciers. The glaciers gradually shrank to their present size as the weather warmed. Here we can see a flowing glacier:

Arete

A sharp ridge. These were formed by two glaciers digging away at opposites sides of a mountain.

Cirque

A semicircular shape that was formed when a glacier started high up the mountain, then scoured back into it.

Horn

A pointy peak where several glaciers have dug away on all sides of a mountain and left a horn-shaped peak.

Pass

A natural low spot in a ridge. Mark guided his team to a pass after their truck got stuck in the snow. It is much easier to walk through the mountains using these low areas.

As the glaciers very slowly flowed down the mountains, they gouged out the rock and dragged pieces with them. At the end of the last ice age, the ice began melting away. Now we can see the shapes left behind by these glaciers. Here are some of the features you might see in mountain areas shaped by glaciation. This picture shows a receding glacier:

U-shaped valley

Glaciers are heavy and slow moving, gouging out everything in their path. When they have melted away, a valley left behind is in the shape of a U. Valleys made by rivers are V-shaped, so you can tell whether a valley was made by ice or a river.

Hanging valley

Glaciers come in different sizes. Little ones make little valleys and big ones make big valleys. If a small glacier joins a big one, it flows into it. After the ice has melted, what is left is a little valley joining a big valley. Often there is a sharp drop, and this is where a waterfall might occur.

Grooves

Long scratches etched into the mountain, formed by glaciers dragging rocks and gravel along.

Learning what these features look like on a map will help you learn what an area looks like in life, and how best to hike through it.

MOVING THROUGH SNOW

Driving

Be prepared! All cars should have an emergency kit that includes a fully charged cell phone, a blanket, a flashlight, first aid supplies, an ice scraper, drinking water, and something to eat. If you get stuck and have to wait for rescue, you can be comfortable.

Snow tires and snow chains grip the snow to keep the car from slipping.

Snow tires sometimes have small metal spikes.

Snow chains wrap around the tire.

Walking through snow

For thousands of years, people who live in deep snowy areas have worn snowshoes. Snowshoes are wide and flat. This spreads a person's weight over a larger area than walking shoes and stops you from sinking into deep snow. Try the experiment opposite with some sand.

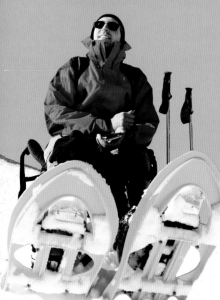

Push your finger into soft sand. It's easy, isn't it? Now push the palm of your hand into the sand. It's not as easy because you have a bigger area to push into the sand.

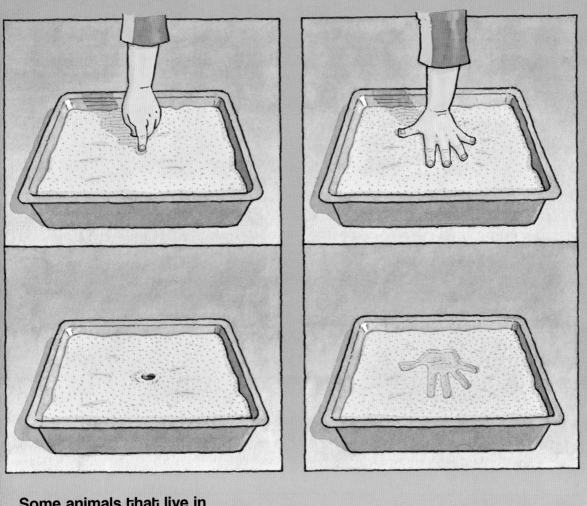

Some animals that live in snowy areas have natural snowshoes. Look at the feet of this snowshoe hare.

First American edition published in 2009
by Boxer Books Limited.

Distributed in the United States and Canada by
Sterling Publishing Co., Inc.
387 Park Avenue South, New York, NY 10016-8810

First published in Great Britain in 2009
by Boxer Books Limited.
www.boxerbooks.com

The illustrations were prepared using ink and watercolor paints on watercolor paper.
The text is set in Adobe Garamond, Coolvetica and Impact.

ISBN 13: 978-1-905417-96-4

1 3 5 7 9 10 8 6 4 2

Printed in China

All of our papers are sourced from managed forests and renewable resources